THE KITTEN STORIES

A Nest for a Kitten

Stephen Jackson

PAGETURNER
PRESS AND MEDIA

Printed in the United States of America

Library of Congress Control Number: 2019909460
ISBN: Softcover   978-1-64376-270-8
              eBook   78-1-64376-271-5

Republished by: PageTurner, Press and Media LLC
Publication Date: 07/15/2019

To order copies of this book, contact:

PageTurner, Press and Media
Phone: 1-888-447-9651
order@pageturner.us
www.pageturner.us

A Nest for a Kitten

"I don't believe it. I flat-out don't believe it, Jack." Stephen Jackson pushed away the document he had been scrutinizing. "Your numbers don't agree with mine. Where the hell did we lose nine hundred thousand dollars?"

Jack grimaced, careful to face out the window and away from his client. Then he spun around in his chair to face Stephen. "We didn't *lose* the money. I have been doing your books—your firm's books—since you had a firm. You asked for this meeting, so the entire team that works on the Jackson and Partners account is here. But we need to face facts: you are going to have to cancel that planned expansion. The money just isn't there; it never was. The account looks full now, but when we finish with payroll, taxes, the holiday party you have already contracted for … it's not there. The numbers are what they are. You could take a loan—"

"No." Stephen's open hand smacked the table as he stood up to look out the window. The three accountants and Jack McMaster, owner of McMaster and Sons, CPA, each flinched at the report of his hand on the wooden tabletop. Two did, actually. The third accountant shifted

1

in her seat, her eyes glued to their client, the hottest attorney in a city made for attorneys. "I didn't build this practice by going into debt. If we can't afford it, we can't."

"That's what I am telling you, Steve," Jack said, leaning forward in his chair. "Maybe you were banking on receipts that have not yet come in; I'm not sure. I called the team together at your request. Just tell us what you want to do."

The thirty-eight-year-old attorney looked at the other people at the table in the accountants' office, making sure to meet them eye to eye as he spoke. "Danny, we have worked together before, and I would like you to look at the income side," Steve said. "Sheryl, I don't think we have ever met, but I know we have talked on the phone—I recognize your voice. Take a look at the pretax values and tax payments; maybe we projected paying less than what we paid. If that is where the error lies, I need to correct our procedures with you." Without missing a beat, the trim, nearly six-foot lawyer continued with his booming voice, not even noticing McMaster standing and starting to speak.

"And you, Miss …? I don't believe we have worked together before?" His eyebrows rose as the lovely woman blushed and started to speak, but finally McMaster was able to get to his feet.

"Steve, this is Megan Murphy. She is new to your account, but a crackerjack accountant. Miss Murphy, you have heard his world-famous voice for the last hour, so let me introduce you to Stephen Jackson—one of DC's most successful attorneys, and one of our best clients. Now—"

Without giving Jack so much as a chance to conclude, Stephen's voice just rode over Jack's, talking to the pretty brunette. "Miss Murphy, I need you to change your schedule for today. Stay here with me and go through the projected cost figures. They just look wrong to me. We can have the files brought in here." Then, as if remembering where he was, he turned, almost sheepishly, to McMaster. "That is, Jack, if this is all okay with you. It occurs to me that this is your firm, not mine."

McMaster, rising to the obvious invitation, responded with a smile and a broad, sweeping gesture. "No, Steve, today this is your firm, this conference room is your office, and Miss Murphy here is your assistant. Megan dear, you *can* change your schedule, can't you?" The way he asked the question made it clear that there was really no alternative.

The brunette smiled prettily and answered, if a little breathlessly, by saying, "Of course, sir; there is absolutely nothing more important to me than satisfying Mr. Jackson." Belatedly realizing that her words were not quite proper, she stammered out a quick save. "Satisfying him that the … the report is accurate, that the project is just too expensive."

Stephen quirked an eyebrow at her and gave a focused look but did not think anything further of it.

Three hours later found the two of them nearly swallowed by paper—paper on the table, paper on the floor, paper everywhere. Fundamentally, Stephen was convinced that the error lay somewhere in projected costs, which is why he had elected to stay with the new girl, Megan. Lord, she was a pretty little thing. And he was intrigued. Every time he demanded a service, called someone in for a special question, she seemed to wet her parted lips and stare—not at the person he was addressing, but at him. Maybe she had just never met an egotistical attorney before?

By 5:00 p.m. Megan was shifting in her seat. Again. There was a meeting set for 5:15 in the very conference room she was in; everyone who had started together would get back together and discuss their findings. Steve knew for a fact that they were not going to finish their part of the review. Almost eight hundred pages of line items had been reviewed. He remarked to her that he hadn't realized how things had

3

grown, yet still no errors had shown up. There was no way they were going to finish special projects in time.

Finally, he put down his pen, rubbed his eyes, and turned to her. "Megan Murphy, if I were the priest of the Catholic school you almost certainly attended and you squirmed like that during one of my lectures, I would flip that skirt up, down your panties, and redden that bottom of yours. We only have fifteen minutes or so. Go to the bathroom before the others get back, if you like. I have been pushing both of us. I will finish off these projected employee bonuses, and then we can hope someone else knows what's wrong."

If he noticed it took her two tries to get up out of her seat, he didn't say anything about it. As he turned back to the next black binder, she steadied herself on the back of the straight chair, murmured that she would be right back, and hurried for the exit. Anyone watching would once again have congratulated Jackson on his perceptive skills: she headed right for the bathroom and entered one of the stalls—but not to pee, although her panties did come down as fast as her skirt went up.

Oh God, she thought to herself as her hands plunged between her thighs. She *wished* she had to go to the bathroom. It had never been like this for her. Every time he looked at her with those incredible eyes, she felt faint … and then he would tell her to do something. She could deal with his requests … but God … the man did know how to command. She sank back on the toilet, her fingers rapidly rolling her rock-hard clit, anxious to just get some relief and get back. Dear heavens, when he had taken off his jacket, put it over the straight-backed chair he sat down on, and removed his silver cufflinks so he could roll up his sleeves … she could see herself right over his lap. She had not felt this way since college—and then, it was self-induced.

Jesus, I do need to find myself a man. But no one ever tells you what you are going to do; they ask you. I don't want to make the decisions. I don't want to make the rules. I want to follow them as best I can, knowing because he *made them, they must be right. It was so much easier being my daddy's little girl. But where do you find a daddy for a twenty-two-year-old college graduate—size five or no?*

She closed her eyes and pictured him again in that straight-backed chair … and came, hard, almost painfully. Exhausted emotionally, but ready to concentrate, she went to draw up her panties, but they were soaked. Small wonder. It would be like pulling on a wet bathing suit, only worse. She took them off, rolled them up, and stuffed them in her purse. It was 5:13.

As she reentered the conference room, Stephen was pacing again, this time with all of the members present, other than her, from the meeting that had started the day. She slid into her chair, only then wondering if the soft material of her skirt would cling to every fold of her skin without her panties, and resolving to be the last person out of the conference room, or even out of her chair. She put her hands together and focused on what the fascinating man who was their client was saying.

"… still don't see it, Jack. Danny, your numbers summary matches mine within a few thousand dollars. I just don't see there being much chance of a significant error." He put his foot up on a chair and looked across at the heavyset blonde, Sheryl. "I don't have any tax numbers, Sheryl; Dawn is not in today, and I cannot get online through your firewall. I have no idea what your tax projections are based on, but looking at your summary, I don't see any tax liability that in one line item is going to come close to nine hundred thousand dollars. Together, sure, we are looking at millions … but I don't think it's likely that multiple mistakes of that significance happened."

McMaster stood up. "Well, I am glad you haven't lost complete confidence in us."

"I didn't say that either, Jack. I do want to find that error. I know it's an error; your numbers cannot be right. When we find it, we can make the decision of what to do next. But it's got to be in projected expenses.

Opening an office cannot cost nearly a million more than we thought. There are more line entries to run down on projections than the other two sectors taken together. Miss Murphy and I have just not finished with that. What I would like to do, Jack, if it's okay with you, is finish up with Megan here tonight and meet with just you in the morning. We can figure out what, if anything, needs to be done after that."

Megan had been listening, and she was struck almost numb by his request. Alone with him? After everyone had gone? She wasn't sure if she wanted that or wanted to run screaming down the hall. Every time she watched him move, her nipples crinkled a little more. And when he turned to her and told her what to do, what to consider ... she wanted to purr. She was so used to being asked "Do you think this?" or "Do you think that?" She hated that part of her job—and that part of her life. But without anyone else ... and she was hungry.

It was as if he'd read her mind, his hazel eyes focusing down on her tightly. "I will even throw in dinner, Miss Murphy—Megan. I don't starve the troops unless I know they will not survive till morning."

She pondered his comment for a minute, not sure if she should worry or not; his brilliant smile soon decided it for her.

Jack looked relieved. "Splendid. Sounds like a course of action. Danny, Sheryl—let's get out of here and let the two of them get to work. Stephen, let's say ten a.m. tomorrow?" It was clear to everyone in the room, including Stephen, that McMaster was overjoyed that a decision on whether to question his services by a principal client had been put off, and he just wanted to keep it that way.

"Sure, Jack. See you then." Stephen sat back down at the table, pulling the pile of papers under the label "projected costs of new employee retention" to him. Then he looked across the table at Megan and began to make some notes. "Miss Murphy—Megan—get me the table of multiplier values on employee retention rates by geographic region, please. Oh, and no, it was not lost on me that we did not give you a vote on whether you would stay to help me. Is that an inconvenience?"

Damn, she loved working with him. She gave a small start as she realized she wished he would command her to do something more intimate than "get the multiplier values." "I will get the table. And no, sir, it's no inconvenience at all. Although, if it is all the same to you, Mr. Jackson, I would rather eat early and come back. Breakfast was fast and hours ago." Now how was she going to handle this? The paper he wanted was down at the end of the long conference table. There was no alternative; she was going to have to stand up and walk away from him. *Just wait till he focuses back on the paper …*

Stephen smiled to himself as he caught himself trying to study the papers with one eye and the young accountant with the other. Damn, but she intrigued him. Cute, sexy—her smile knocked him out. And she didn't seem to mind being told what to do, his normal operating style, rather than letting him know she should be asked. No equal rights issues. As she walked to the end of the table, his eyes focused on her—the way she moved. Something was different. He smiled, but the smile never escaped his eyes. Now if only his guess on the multiplier values were right … but it *would* add up to $900,000! He thought about trying not to be obvious, and then he shrugged and watched the brunette as she turned to bring him the multiplier tables. He was right. Now he would have to find out why. The hours the two of them had spent together had told him enough to make him certain she was on edge—excited, and a little bit flustered. He hoped that her excitement was positive, and his fault.

"Is there something wrong, sir?" Her pupils dilated under his intense scrutiny, and Stephen supposed it could be with alarm rather than excitement. One word from him to McMaster tomorrow and she could be on the way to the branch office in Yazoo City, Mississippi, doing the endless books for Mississippi Chemical Co., McMaster's oldest and number-one client. Or his word could put her out on the street.

"What? Oh, no, Miss Murphy—nothing at all. I was just trying to decide whether you would prefer fish or beef or vegetables. No, there is nothing wrong. Thanks for the tables." Reaching his hand out to take the requested paper from her, he deliberately brushed the back of her hand, looking for a tightening of her smile—and he saw it. Definitely, there would be things to talk about at dinner.

As she turned back to the stacks she still had to go through, he pulled out his cell phone. "Edward, how are you? Yes, of course it's Stephen … Yes, I am fine. And you are right, so I am going to give you that chance … Tonight? Seven? Could we do … wait."

Putting his hand over the cell phone, he cleared his throat to catch her attention. "You said you were hungry, kitt … Miss Murphy. Would six thirty at Citronelle do? It's five after six now."

She didn't have to say anything. At her wide-eyed look of amazement and a nod, he turned back to the cell phone.

"Yes, Edward? Six thirty would do us better than seven. My accountant will be with me; you know how they are!" Rolling his eyes at the startled girl, he concluded his chat with the maître d' and then turned back to her. "I think, Megan, that it makes sense to stop where we are, stroll the couple of blocks to the restaurant, and then finish up here after. That should get you home about ten p.m." Without another word, he folded the table he had asked for and slid it into the inside pocket of his jacket. He went through the process, fascinating to Megan, of rolling his shirt sleeves down and refastening the cufflinks, and he then put the jacket on.

Megan was amazed but enthralled. He had never asked her where or what she wanted to eat. God, how she loved that. But she had to speak up.

"Sir? Mr. Jackson, sir? That sounds heavenly, but … I can't afford

Citronelle, sir. And it's not something I can really authorize on the firm's card. I have only been here about six months and—"

"Never mind, Megan. I don't recall asking you to pay. Even if you were ugly, four foot eight and 295 pounds, sixty-five years old, and a man, I would still pay. I asked you. As it is"—he offered her a smile, his first true smile of the day that she thought really brightened his face—"you don't look a day over twenty-three."

She debated a split second and then decided she could risk it. "Damn, I was hoping you had noticed I was not a man."

At his laugh, she stood up, nervous about her appearance but totally unable to do a thing about it. He put one hand gently on her back, and they left for the restaurant. As they walked the block and a half, talking about the warm fall weather, she wondered if the skin on her back would ever stop burning.

Dinner passed in a whirl for Megan. Never before had she been in a place where she was fussed over, consulted on every aspect of her meal. And when she had expressed her desire that there should have been one more of the appetizers, an entire dish was brought out immediately. She realized that it was all for him; he knew everyone by name. When he had told the wine steward that they would not be drinking that night as they had more work to do, she thought the sommelier was going to cry. And Stephen had been as charming and interesting as she had known he would be. She simply listened to his endless stream of stories and anecdotes, interjecting her childhood when he asked. She had kind of stammered when he asked her, out of midair, what her favorite color was—why did it matter?—but in the spirit of the moment, she told him. "Light blue, just like my suit."

"It's a gorgeous suit, Megan. It … well … it suits you." His smile warmed her from inside out. He had called over the maître d'—the Edward he had called from their office—and he in turn brought a beautiful woman from the desk over. Megan had absolutely no idea what he was whispering to her about, but she smiled, nodded, and then turned back to him, one eyebrow raised.

"Oh, I don't know. A five, I think." And with that, she was gone.

Megan had declined dessert, but she accepted cappuccino. As they waited for the coffees, his eyes suddenly went distant. She did not know what was wrong; it looked for all the world like he had simply gone away. Then he pulled out the table of figures he had brought with him, scanned it for a few seconds, and turned back to her, folding the table away. "Sorry, Megan, my business is a distraction that keeps me from talking to the most beautiful woman in the restaurant, who is sitting right across the table from me." And then he really did turn a smile on her. She pressed her thighs together under the table and prayed that the night would end so she could go home and dream about what might have been.

"I think, Megan … that I have changed my mind. I want dessert after all. But it's not on the menu. I think maybe you can help me."

"Sir, I am not sure I understand. But you know that we will do everything we can for you. You are a really important client to us. Hands down, our favorite." And she put her palms down on the table, illustrating her point.

He covered her small hand with one of his own, a warm drape trapping her, the heat rapidly building there. "This has nothing to do with McMaster & Sons, or Jackson and Partners, or any silly nine hundred thousand dollars, Megan. This has to do with just you and me. What I want. What I will ask for. What I think is appropriate for you. I have spent all day with you, young lady, and made some judgments."

She thought her heart was going to leap out of her chest and splash the coffee that was just arriving. She closed her eyes momentarily, convinced that given the failure during the day to discover the source of the discrepancy, he was about to tell her she was not to work on his matters again. And that would be the end.

"What I want for dessert, Megan, is really very simple. I want you to remove your panties and place them for me here on the table."

For a moment, so convinced was she that she was about to hear words of doom, she didn't even understand what he had said. Then she replayed his voice in her head, and her eyes flew wide. Her face grew bright red. And then another thought flashed through her head, and she uttered a soft groan.

"Oh, sir ... Mr. Jackson ... I can't do that. I ... I am an employee ... and I can't do that."

His grip tightened on her hand, which he had never let go of. His bright smile was back. "I know that, Megan ... Megan ... there must be an equally fearsome Irish name to fit between Megan and Murphy, dear?"

She was having trouble jumping from subject to subject, her mind still on what was not underneath her skirt. So she automatically responded by saying, "Kathleen. Megan Kathleen. But only when I am in trouble." She offered a fleeting smile and then gently tried to extract her hand from his.

He only tightened his grip. "Megan Kathleen, I know you can't do as I ask. I have known since you came back from the bathroom, dear. It has nothing to do with the fact that you are an employee of the firm I do business with, now does it?"

She shook her head, her cheeks glowing red. Tears began to leak from the corners of her eyes. "I am sorry," she whispered, and she reached for her purse. "I will just go home now, sir ... I will resign tomorrow. Thank you—thank you for a wonderful dinner." As she tried to stand up, he pulled her hand toward him, effectively putting her back down on the banquette. For Megan, in her embarrassment, the world had shrunk to their table—to his face, and his strong hand holding hers.

"Young lady," Stephen said, "I am not terribly used to being disobeyed. You may well resign tomorrow; that is yet to be determined.

But you will not resign or be fired because you chose not to wear panties to dinner; you are much too smart and talented to have your career ended by a choice of underwear that was entirely yours to make. I told you I knew you could not honor my request. The only issue we have to resolve right now is whether your panties are somewhere with you, so that you *can* give them to me—or perhaps you left them back at the office?"

"Oh God, sir ... please don't ... please." He had said "smart and talented." Did he mean it? She was so lost already; what did it matter? She would be lucky to get the Mississippi Chemical assignment. She opened her purse and took out the pair of panties without saying a word. Her mortification only increased when he opened them out on the table, and began to press the fabric between his fingers, sliding them over the small garment. He reached the crotch and smiled at her. "For me, Megan?"

She could only nod, nod hard. When she got embarrassed, she tended to put her head down and nod—the more she felt about something, the harder the nod.

"How utterly charming. And now, dear, I think we need to get back." He gathered up her precious underwear and put it in his jacket pocket. He stood up, offered her his hand, and continued as if nothing at all had happened. She could not have been more embarrassed had she lost her bowels right there in DC's fanciest restaurant. She glanced furtively around to see if there was anyone she recognized, and then she gave a small laugh. No one she knew *ever* ate there. She really had no choice but to take his hand and go on back. Certain that once they got back to the office he would tell her to go home, she could do nothing but follow. She would have followed him anywhere, if only he had wanted her.

He stopped to sign the check at the front desk, and the woman who had come by earlier to their table handed him a small bag. He accepted the package and then grinned at his companion. "Lunch for tomorrow."

She hardly noticed the walk back. Her eyes watched him but did not see. He seemed unchanged from when they had left the office. She thought about what he had said. "Talented"? But he had seen her come back from the bathroom. *Oh God,* she thought. It wasn't when she walked away ... when she walked back. "Sir. Mr. Jackson? It was the curls that gave me away?"

He knew precisely what she meant. "Yes, Megan. I suspected when you walked to the end of the table to get the chart. The skirt seemed to drape on your skin more closely. But when you walked toward me, the smooth fabric that had been there was replaced with the stippling of your lovely body. But you do trim it beautifully, dear, if that is any consolation."

It wasn't. She thought wildly that she was lucky there were no manholes in their area, or she would slip right down one. Then his hands were on her shoulders, turning her to look at him. One hand went under her chin so that their eyes met. "It's important that you listen to me, Megan Kathleen." At her blink, he nodded. "Megan Kathleen is reserved for the moments when you might be in trouble, right?" She told herself she would not cry, pressing her eyes closed and then opening them to his hazel ones once more, acknowledging that he was right.

"Good. Then Megan Kathleen, we are going to go back upstairs to that very messy conference room. We are going to find the answer to the problem that has eluded us all afternoon. And then we will make a determination as to what to do about you. And perhaps—perhaps not—what to do about us. But I want you to understand something: I will not have you fired. Do you understand me?"

Her heart slowed a bit. Was there a way out of this horrid trap? He wouldn't fire her. But he had said he would give a report to McMaster ...

and he would. But he had *also* said "Talented." She took a deep breath and said simply, "Yes, sir. I am happy to do as you direct."

"That, Miss Murphy, may be the most perceptive thing you have said all day."

She steeled herself, and they went back up to the conference room. He pulled one of the straight-backed chairs out away from the table … and just left it there. That puzzled her, but he said nothing about it. He laid his bag from the restaurant down and then pulled the stack of papers over and hunted through it for a few moments. She sat there with her hands folded on the table, waiting for instructions and watching as he traced something down a piece of paper in front of him. Finally he looked up. "Megan, come here, please; I need your help double-checking something."

She came around the table, now acutely conscious of how she looked beneath the thin material of the skirt of her suit, and stood at his right shoulder beside the paper-heavy table. "Megan, double-check the multiplier that the table says to use on the cost of office preparation in Georgia, using our office in DC as a base. What is the figure we are supposed to use?"

She wanted to cheer; this was something she was certain she could respond to. She knew the answer, but she double-checked anyway. "It's one, sir; there is no difference in pricing."

"Right you are, Miss Murphy. Now, confirm for me, if you would, the multiplier value recited in the McMaster projection." He handed her the sheet of paper he had pulled out of the stack on their return.

Sliding her finger down her firm's projection, she gave a small gasp. "Oh my God; it's one point nine! And that means—"

"Exactly, Megan Kathleen. Since we used the one-million-dollar cost for the DC opening as the baseline, your projection was precisely nine hundred thousand dollars more than it should have been. Which means the Atlanta office is affordable. Which is fundamentally good news—a piece of news I would not have been alerted to without your assistance, dear. Watching you took my mind off the specific numbers.

"Now, that's the good news. And McMaster will be thrilled. But there are some things yet to resolve, aren't there, young lady?"

When he stopped talking, he turned to look up at her to see her tears streaming down her cheeks. She didn't trust herself to speak; she could only nod. Stephen continued. "The individual responsible for inserting the wrong multiplier value into my firm's projection is a beautiful brunette with green eyes and the Irish name of Megan Kathleen Murphy, isn't she, dear?" His voice could not have been more quiet.

He stood up to stretch and sat back down in the straight-backed chair he had earlier pulled out. "A long afternoon, Megan. I want to be fair about this, dear. If I tell McMaster what happened, you will lose not only your job, but your career, won't you?"

She finally found a small voice. "Yes, sir. I just … just want to say … that if I had to end my accounting career early, I am so glad I got a chance to work with you … and dinner … even dessert, was wonderful." Head down, the young girl turned to head for the door.

Crack! He had slapped his open hand down on the table to get her attention, the same tactic he had used so effectively earlier that day. She stopped in her tracks. "I said *if*, young lady. I cannot let this action go … unless you receive some discipline. If I tell Jack, the discipline will be exactly as you say. But Jack is not the only disciplinarian, Megan Kathleen." He patted his lap while sitting on the chair. "Come here, girl."

She walked toward him, but her face showed complete confusion. As she reached his chair, he put one hand on her hip and looked up at her. "You can resign, and save yourself the ugly dressing-down from Jack, Megan. Or you can receive exactly what the table received, five times. The choice is yours, young lady." Stephen paused, his eyes never wavering from hers. "If you accept your discipline from me as you should, there will be … a difference."

"Sir?"

"Dammit, girl. You must do exactly as I say or quit tonight. Do as I say, and your life opens up again. Which will it be? You are out of time."

"Sir, if you will find some way to avoid my termination … I will do anything you ask."

"Good, now not a word out of you." She had expected anything, but she never dreamed his first action would be to undo her belt and lower the side zipper on her skirt. "Oh, Mr. Jackson—"

He did not wait for her to finish but grabbed her hair with his left hand and roughly pulled the accountant over his lap, naked from the waist except for thigh-highs and heels. "Oh my God … sir—"

Quicker than thought, the rolled-up pair of panties from his pocket was in her mouth, muffling her cries. He gathered her wrists in his one hand and pressed them down on her back. She was off balance, unprepared for—

Smack! His open hand impacted directly on the center of her bottom. The burn on her skin was immediate, but that was not where she was focused. The same impact triggered something else inside her— something she had searched for—and it brought her wet instantly. "Oh God" was all she could mumble into the gag.

Again and again and again, his hand fell on one cheek, the other, both. The stinging was at a constant level, but her fever pitch rose faster as she began unconsciously to move against him, seeking release in a tortured emotional and physical state. "That's four, Megan. I promised you five." He stopped a minute to run his finger along her clearly wet slit. His touch pushed her over the edge, her tummy and pussy spasming and spasming. And then his final stroke fell, just at the center of the undercurve of her bottom, directly above her swollen slit.

"Ahhh *Godddd!*" She ejected the panties from her mouth with the

16

scream of release and then fell silent against his lap, shuddering and whimpering with the violence of her orgasm.

At length, he gently lifted her and held her to him so that her red bottom was off his lap, her body secure in his arms. "Megan? Megan Kathleen?"

Her eyes were still glazed, and she nodded her head against his chest, taken back to the last time she felt secure, controlled, guided, and protected in a man's arms. "Yes, Daddy?" After a moment, she realized what she had said and jerked upright. To her amazement, he simply pressed her head back against his chest. "That's all right, kitten; I like Daddy better than Mr. Jackson anyhow. I wasn't sure, Megan, how you would react, but I think you are okay. I have no need to consult with Jack in the morning, dear. But … I do have a need."

Sitting on his lap, she suddenly realized how hard he was inside his pants. She involuntarily licked her lips and then, smiling shyly at him, said, "May I … Daddy?"

"I think so, kitten. You get dessert too, after all." Without another word, she slid to her knees between his, unzipped him, and pulled his cock out of his pants as if she were receiving the Holy Grail from God himself. She teased the end with her tongue and then, at his growl of "Megan," began to suck in earnest. He had fought for control with the vivacious girl all afternoon; she wasn't the most beautiful, the smartest, or the most educated woman he had ever spent time with, but she reached him in a spot where no one else had.

It took only moments before he was pounding deep into her throat, arching his back—and yet, after each gag, she came back for more. His eyes closed as he exploded in her with a great *"Arrrggghh."* When he came to his senses, she was cleaning around the edges. She smiled up at him, still on her knees, and he reached down and wiped a droplet of saliva and cum off the corner of her mouth. With that, she leaned against his knees.

The soft vibration he felt puzzled him for a moment, until he realized she was purring with contentment. He ruffled her hair lightly and murmured, "You're home, kitten. I have a nest for you."

Shortly, he drew her back into his arms, taking and sharing a soft kiss or three. "You are still going to have to meet with Jack and me at ten tomorrow, Megan."

The girl was wounded immediately. He would have laughed but for the tears that poured forth. "I thought … I thought …" was all she could stammer.

"Oh, Megan … not to be yelled at. To resign, dear. You cannot be my kitten and work for Jack. It just wouldn't do. We will stay at my apartment in the city tonight, and tomorrow, after the meeting, we can see about getting enough of your stuff—until I can have you moved in to my house by the end of the week." She looked at him in wonderment, and then she took his head between both hands and kissed him long and hard. "Are you sure, sir?"

"One thing you will learn, Megan Kathleen Murphy, is that I am sometimes wrong, but I am always sure."

She slid off his lap and bent to pick up her skirt. "Megan," Stephen said, his voice stern, "you can't walk into my apartment building like that! What would the doorman think?" He reached into the bag from the restaurant and brought out a filmy pair of light blue panties, exactly the color of her suit. "Another reason for dining at Citronelle, Megan— they are in Georgetown Square, a wonderful shopping mall. Size five, I presume?" Megan accepted the gift and slipped on her new panties, and her skirt, and then she slipped her hand into his.

Megan looked around the room. "Shouldn't we clean up?"

"Megan, dear … you don't work here anymore. And I am a client. We can surprise Jack in the morning. I am sure the fact that I have decided to move forward with the expansion plans will cover the cost of all this paper." He picked up the bag and led her toward the door.

"Sir … Daddy? What's in the bag?"

"Why kitten, you *are* full of curiosity," Stephen said. "Lubricant and a probe, dear. I thought we might not get much sleep tonight. Vanessa knows her underwear, and she knows what kittens like." Megan just burrowed into his shoulder, suppressing small shudders of excitement. As they were leaving, she reached out to turn off the lights, leaving behind a pile of papers and, on the floor, a very wet, very rumpled pair of women's panties—size five.

A Lesson for a Kitten

The clock by the bedside clicked as "3:00 a.m." popped up on the digital display. Megan chewed her lip as she listened to Stephen's deep breathing. She was always amazed at his ability to sleep every night. He joked and told her it was because his heart was pure. Whatever the reason, the soft, low sounds coming from his chest—and the matching vibrations, if they were spooned with her back to his body—were usually guaranteed to put her to sleep. And she had to admit that she had never slept as soundly as she did in his arms, more often than not her warmed bottom buried against him. But not tonight; she thought and fretted all through the short hours of the night. Last night had left her in tears—quiet ones, and ones that he had kissed away and told her did not matter—but she had never failed him in the bed, and she did not intend to make it a habit now.

It had started innocently enough. She had been dying for a spanking, wanting one. It made her feel safe and secure. In his arms, over his lap, she really had no cares in the world. It was an extension of him. He did not rule her life—she was not his submissive—but she knew, in her heart and soul, that she was his; that he would guide her life from the day they met to the end of time. And she never felt more alive, more certain of her place in his life, than while and immediately after she was being spanked—and, of course, afterward: in his arms, in his bed, in his bath. It was all part of the incredible world she had entered. She had wandered into it quite unaware and innocent of it, knowing only that her life up until the day he came into the accounting office she worked at had been grey; it lacked the color she wanted. The men and women in her life were just … there. No one to reach out and bring her to the table of life.

Then he had sat down in the conference room with her, going through data and paper, searching through the files she had made for the error he was certain existed—an error she had made without knowing it. Certain of himself, and her, he had argued, directed, made decisions, and even arranged for dinner in the way she had always dreamed her man would. And when, in the depths of the moment, she had had to remove her panties to take care of a growing passion, and had not been able to replace them, he kept the knowledge of that to himself, until they were alone and private.

She had despaired of losing her job, after he had made it clear, even to her, that it was her mistake that had led to a wrong conclusion about his firm's ability to expand. To her passionate delight, it was another instant decision on his part. He simply took her, lowered her skirt, and put her over his knee and paddled her. She came hard against his knee and, in the aftermath, found the place she had been looking for all her adult life. She moved in with him that night and had never left.

And he spanked her now, just as he had that first night eight months earlier. Sometimes he spanked her just because they both enjoyed it, sometimes because she needed it. The previous night, she had just wanted it, even though she knew he was distracted by some case at work. Megan liked to shower at night; it left her morning free to get her hair and face in order and handle the day. He had a rule: whenever she pulled on a new pair of panties, she had the obligation to tell him or show him, or both, what they were. It was one of a small set of rules he used to remind her that she was his. She had sat with him as he worked but had been unable to distract him from the business before him with any great success. He would absentmindedly kiss her, caress her, and then turn his attention back to the heavy files on his desk. She knew being jealous of a stack of papers was absurd, but she could not simply forget about it. So she devised a small plan.

She knew that of all her panties, he liked the powder-blue bikinis the best. She showered and trimmed, put on her most exciting perfume, drew on the panties he loved, and threw a light, short nightgown over it. As provocative as she was going to be that night, she slipped on a pair of mules to put extra sway in her walk, paraded into the study where he was still at work, and simply whispered in his ear, "I don't want to bother you, Stephen dear, so I am just going to bed. I am all ready but will leave the hallway light on." Giving him a small kiss, she turned, a smile on her face, and hoped for the result she wanted. She had one foot out in the hallway when his voice, in the low tones that always shivered her skin, came. Her smile faded.

"Excuse me a minute, young lady; I think you forgot something." She turned, thrilled that her ploy was working so well, and gave him a look of pure innocence.

"I don't think so, Stephen. Everything is taken care of, and I am headed off to bed."

"Don't even move." He got up from his chair, taking a moment to put a pencil in the file where he was reading, and came to her in two short strides. She knew she was in more trouble than she had planned on when, rather than lifting her nightgown, he simply ripped it at the top and let it slide to the floor. "I think, young lady, that you knew that you broke the rule, and that you did it deliberately. You did it because you think you are not getting attention this evening, and this is your way of finding a path to my lap. The panties are lovely, Megan—as pretty as when I gave them to you in the conference room where we first met. And you know it. You succeeded in getting my attention, Megan. Did you do it deliberately?" He lifted her chin with one finger so that she was looking directly into his eyes.

"Yes, sir. I am not sure why. I just … just need you, I guess."

He kissed her softly on the forehead and then took her by the wrist and led her to a corner of his study where a wall met the built-in bookshelves. "Wait here for me, Megan. Do not move a muscle; keep your hands at your sides. You have succeeded in distracting me, but my work is not yet done."

She only began to get a glimmer of what he had in mind for her when he slid the panties down to midway along her thighs and then left her standing there. Halfway down was not a good sign—discipline, not play. Without another word, he stepped away from her, and she heard his footsteps head down the hallway. As she stood there, even with no one in the room, tears began to gather in her eyes. She had overplayed her scheme, and all she knew was that she was not going to get what she had hoped for. Finally, she heard his footsteps coming back up the hallway that led to their bedroom and bathroom, and she took a deep breath, steeling herself for the sharper spanking she knew must be coming: a shoe, perhaps, or a paddle.

"Good, Megan." She heard Stephen kneel behind her. With her eyes fixed on the corner where he had placed her, she desperately wanted to turn and face him, but she was held in place by his command. "Now," he said, "keep your eyes to the front, please."

To her amazement, the next thing she knew, his finger was in her anus, gently easing lubricant in and around her. He had never ever done that to her before. She had played with it before she met him, but never beyond a "this is how it feels" kind of thing. She had desperately wanted to explore her own bottom, or more precisely, have him explore it, but she was very much afraid of it, too.

"Kittens who sometimes forget or innocently break a rule, Megan, get spanked. Kittens that set out to break a rule, who do it deliberately, get corner time. After that, well, we will see. Now, as long as you absolutely keep your hands at your side, young lady, your strokes will stay the same. For the first five minutes, this is all you will feel." She would have jumped, had his hand not been on her, as he easily inserted into her bottom a small plastic bead. Truly, it was barely big enough to be retained by her. Standing there, she thought she could force it out, but she knew that would be forbidden. She shifted uncertainly in her mules as he made sure the bead was secured. He then said to her quietly, "You will recite, Megan Kathleen, the following words, until I change the bead in your bottom: I have been a bad girl, and am being punished. Slowly and clearly. Can you do that?" Finally, he stood and turned her head to look at him.

At the look in his eyes, stern and unhappy, the tears that had been gathering burst forth, flowing onto her cheeks. As she raised her hand to wipe them away, he caught it, and then the other. "You are to leave these at your side, kitten. You may not touch your face, wipe your tears, or blow your nose. Now, do as I have asked of you." He gently turned her back to the corner. She thought he had left the room again, but moments later, she heard his voice from farther away. He was, she realized, back at his desk. "Recite, Megan."

And she broke into a monotone repetition of the words he had used to admonish her. When she stopped, his voice sounded. "Again." She began to cry and recite, upset and confused about what was to happen. After some time had passed, he got up from his chair and came over to her. She almost fainted from relief; now the evening could end, and she would be back over his lap. But no. He knelt again, and suddenly, a second, larger bead was in her bottom, pushing the first before it. This one she could not ignore.

"Oh my God—"

"*Recite*," came the command. That was not a voice she could ignore, and she tried to focus on the words that shamed her. But she found it hard to ignore the feelings in her bottom, and she shifted back and forth as the tears continued to flood her face. "There will be no spanking for you tonight, little one, not while I am working. But you will remember this night." Memories of corner time from long ago came to her—always standing, always dreading the end but needing it to come quickly. And unconsciously, she addressed him with a term she had not used since the night they met.

"Yes, Daddy," said a meek voice.

His eyebrow crooked up in surprise, and he smiled at her back at her soft voice and then turned back to his work.

And so it went—the continual command of "Recite" followed by an ever larger bead. The time between beads stretched as well as each one got larger. As he inserted the fifth bead into her, she felt a small cramp and then heard his soft words.

"I do not intend for you to endure more than you physically can, Megan. You have never had anything up your bottom before, have you, kitten?" Her blush blazed on both cheeks and well down on her throat and chest. "Five beads will be the limit you will receive today, then, Megan." She started, suddenly, as he moved the beads inside her; she did not know what to expect next. "Just making sure they were well seated, Megan. Now recite."

And the beautiful brunette did her best to focus on the words she was to recite, and the lesson, but increasingly, she felt the discomfort from the inserted beads. "I … I ha … have be … been a b-b-b-bad girl, and am b-b-being punished." She was new to this and did not quite know how to deal with it. Her shifting must have come to his attention.

"Uncomfortable, Megan?" Stephen asked from across the room.

"Yes, yes. I am sorry, but I really need to … I need to be excused, Daddy. This is something … I can't—"

"Shh, Megan. It's all right. I think the lesson is well started." He had gotten up from the desk and caressed her cheek without her hearing him get up. "The lesson is not finished, Megan, but I think we can bring you some relief. I need you to hold still." She felt his hand on her ass, his firm fingers spreading her a bit and then pulling on the beads—firm, steady pressure, building in her. Then there was a kind of slithering pop as the largest bead came out of her. The noise brought a fiery blush back to her, it being as humiliating as the corner time.

"Oh my God—I am so sorry." In her embarrassment, the beautiful girl sought to cover herself as the remaining beads came out. As Stephen drew her panties off of her completely, she fell to her knees, fresh tears cascading as she tried to hide her face in his leg, seeking his forgiveness.

"Megan, dear, you are my kitten and always will be. I want you to go to the bathroom, dear, and take a moment. When you are collected, simply go to the bedroom and wait for me. Tummy down, Megan."

Minutes later—or hours; she really lost count, being kind of in a haze—she heard his soft footsteps in the bedroom, and then she heard the bed shift as he climbed up on the mattress, kneeling beside her. "I think you know, Megan, that I spend every minute I possibly can with you, that I would much rather hold you than a pen, that I would rather touch you than write a brief. Don't you?"

Not trusting her voice, Megan merely nodded, burying her head in the pillow. "I am certain you know, princess, that the spanking you wanted is not the one you are going to get, but that seems to be the very best way to get your attention." Megan felt herself raised by his hand under her tummy, and he put first one and then two of the big king-size pillows that adorned their bed underneath her. "Now, pretty Miss on the pillows, spread your legs for me." As she allowed herself to be adjusted by his hands, she realized to her horror and embarrassment that she was open and on display, her labia gaping open, her bottom upturned.

"This is your slipper, Megan," he said to her softly, throwing its mate up by her head, which was now turned to one side to look at him. "A slippering is a different kind of a spanking, young lady. I think you won't like it much." And without more, the slipper began to snap onto her skin—*Whap! Snap! Crack!*—one stroke after another. No one stroke was painful, as the slipper was soft and flexible, but stroke after stroke built a heat in her, first in her bottom. Then he moved to her inner thighs, with the comment, "Crimson is red enough for today."

Soon she was crying loudly, begging him to stop. And the barrage of slipper slaps stopped as abruptly as it had started, replaced with his hand over the center of her bottom. His hands were always warm, she knew, but she was shocked how cool his hand seemed, placed on her bottom. "Have you learned today's lesson, kitten? Am I likely to have to deal with an artificial kitten distraction again when I have serious work to complete, and you know that?"

In a voice barely audible, surrounded by sniffles and tears, he heard her say, "No, sir. I am sorry to have been such a distraction." He smiled, for she was a distraction—always, and he was glad of it. And as he had slippered her and then put his hands on her, he had noticed that she was responding with her usual passion. A short pass over her slit with a finger was all they both needed to know she was as wet and ready for him as he was hard for her. "It seems a shame," he said, looking at her bright red bottom and gently fingering her lubricated ass, "to waste such a beautiful setting." He played with her clit with one hand and eased his finger deep into her bottom with the other.

"Stephen?" said her soft voice, "what are you doing? Don't you want me to … well, what *do* you want? I thought you would just enter me, but maybe I could taste you first."

He simply kissed the very warm skin of her bottom and softly said, "Why waste a perfectly warmed, perfectly lubricated, and perfectly beautiful bottom, Megan?"

She wasn't clear about what she needed to do, and as she felt him press against her, she tightened up in fear and expectation. The harder he tried to calm her and relax her, the tighter and more frightened she became. He finally just kissed her warm and long on the lips, lay down on his side, and pulled her to him to snuggle against him—her bottom against his cock, but a simple snuggle.

This left her wide awake, upset, and worried. She had never failed him with her body, with whatever he had asked of her or wanted. How would he react? What would he do? She knew it was simply a foolish fear magnified by the middle of the night, but what if he decided she was not experienced enough for him, not enough woman for him? How could she leave? What would she do? And so she watched the clock click past three o'clock on its way to the sunrise.

The dawn came with Stephen as cheerful as ever, waking her for a long, hard kiss before setting off to work. There was no indication from him that things were going to change—but then there never was; they would just change, and the tide would go out. Biting her fingernails, Megan straightened the house after breakfast and then sat down to read up on anal sex. By the time she got up after lunch, she was, frankly, stupefied. She had never read so much and learned so little. The thing that had impressed her the most was a video of incredible things being forced in a woman's bottom: bottles, fists, pool balls. She had never dreamed people did that sort of thing. And she knew that she could not do that. Dear God, she loved him so, but she could never do some of the things she read about and saw.

She was kind of in a haze about two o'clock when she turned as the door opened, and there he stood, with the half smile that let her know that he was up to something. He had some small bags, and a briefcase stuffed full of work. "I thought, Megan, that we could enjoy the afternoon playing with some things I bought. I put off the appointments, and if I really, really need to, I can do some of this work later." He had totally surprised her. She had put on a pair of comfortable shorts and top, but she had not gotten herself ready. She usually waited until he was likely to be home soon, typically around 6:30, before getting dressed and doing her makeup. She ran to him, partly to keep him from looking at her ratty clothes too long, and gave him a huge hug and tilted her head up for the kiss she knew he would share with her.

"Megan, you look and taste divine. But I wanted to make up for last night. Will you forgive me, kitten? And will you do exactly what I ask, and without asking why? I want to show you how wonderful anal sex can be, kitten. It should have been wonderful last night, but I got too excited. You were just too pretty for me."

She had stopped listening closely when she had hear the words "Will you forgive me"; she had been about to beg of him the very same thing. She simply half melted into his arms, holding tightly onto his body. Her world was not about to end, and for now, that was enough. So it came as a little surprise as he swung an arm behind her knees, his other around her back, and lifted her up off her feet and into his arms. "You have to carry the bags, kitten—and no peeking." Although she was dying to know what was in the bags, there was not enough money in the world to get her to peek; the light in his eyes, after the sleepless night and fretful morning, was all she truly wanted.

Finally in the bedroom, he put the bags on the nightstand, reached for her, and gently undressed her, dropping her shorts and pulling the T-shirt off her head and arms. Then he stripped himself. She knew he was only being considerate, but the pause in the removal of her clothes let her think too long about the plain cotton bra and green bikinis she was wearing—and let her wish she had put something sexier on. Soon he was, as he liked to put it, unwrapping her at last, and he held her, on her knees, by the shoulders at arm's length, studying her intently, until she began to blush.

"You are gorgeous, Megan Kathleen, and I am going to love teaching you new things." With that, he gently turned her. Easing the pillows around, he placed one under her head and two up under her pelvis. It wasn't until his finger gently began to run around the outside of her bottom that she realized she was in exactly the same position as the one he had had her in the previous night. "Shh, Megan. I forgot myself last night. Last night I had only Vaseline for you. Tonight, well, this is called Liquid Silk, princess. I think you will feel the difference." And she could; it was as if her bottom were slippery today, not just gelled up.

She heard one of the shopping bags rustle. "Now, kitten," Stephen said from behind her, "I brought some things home with me. The first is for your bottom, little one, and it's tiny. Not at all like the beads you got last night, even. Now, deep breath, and here we go." Megan felt a small pressure at her anus, but it was mild, and then it was gone. She could feel something in there—it was a stick or something—but if fit in easily. "That is just a rectal thermometer, kitten—something even babies can take right in."

Twisting her head around, she looked back with slitted eyes. "Even I could take a thermometer. I had them when I was a child, you know. Stop playing."

He only smiled at her and said, "You have never had a rectal thermometer placed in you by a man who loves and wants you, Megan." As he said it, his right hand reached out gently and eased a finger up between her spread labia, another finger pressing on her clit. She had not even realized how wet she really was. As he was playing with her, and as she pushed backward for greater contact, he played with the thermometer in her bottom, pulling it out and pushing it in, wiggling it. Completely unexpectedly, she came, in a brief spasm against his finger, her mind focused completely on the sensations in her bottom. She bit her lip and pressed her face into the pillow, aroused and embarrassed, seizing on his finger in her with her muscles. Ever afterward, putting what she insisted on calling a baby thermometer in her would have a centering effect on Megan. More than anything else, it effectively controlled her, focusing her very tightly on her body.

Megan felt Stephen's smile as he kissed her up her back and neck and whispered, "That was a little one, princess. Ready for more?" Almost drunk at the thought, Megan nodded, and he moved back, lubricating her again. "This time, kitten, I have something bigger for you. This is called a plug, honey, and you will feel it for certain." As he talked, she felt a hard, continuous push at her bottom, at the muscle in her anus. His other hand was underneath her, keeping her from pushing away from it. And gradually, she felt something entering her. It felt enormous, although she knew it could not be much larger than the beads he had inserted in her. But it grew and it grew until that was all she could think about.

Even as he began to tease at her wet folds again, she could not help thinking about the thing in her ass, as though it were some dark growth or something. But as it rested in her, at his "It's all the way in, kitten" she began to relax. She *loved* the fullness of it, and when he put a finger in her and pressed against the firmness of the plug through the thin wall of her tissue, she had to bite her lips and then release her excitement in a slow, but loud, moan. "I don't want to bring you fast again, princess, but I want you to get used to the feeling of having something man-shaped inside you, Megan. So I am going to leave it in you while I play with the vegetables."

She had no idea what he was talking about, but he sat up on the edge of the bed, and she watched, curled on her side, taking a quick taste of his hard cock as he pulled out a vegetable peeler and some kind of root. "This is ginger, Megan. Some people think that it can make anal sex very hot—not just sexy, but it makes the tender skin inside you agitated. For other people, it has no impact at all. This is very gentle, but as you can see, I get to peel it away until it is just the size and shape I like it." He had carved it down to a very wide base—much too wide to fit in her, she knew—with a gradual taper. He turned it and showed her that he had left a hard ridge along it. "So that you can feel it pass along your tunnel, Megan, and know exactly where it is."

Stephen put her back on her knees and gently withdrew the plug in her. Even with his care, it still exited with a kind of a loud sighing. *Are all anal toys so noisy?* Megan wondered to herself with her head buried in the pillow. The thought that it was her body making the noise was almost more embarrassing than the thought that she had eagerly had these things stuck up her bottom and was craving more. She wanted to reach down and play, but she knew he wanted this to go on and on, so she contented herself by keeping her hands on her breasts, playing with her nipples, just intensifying the feelings a little.

"Here we go, Megan," was all he said, and then the new sensation of having the carved ginger root gently inserted in her caught her by surprise. "Oh, oh my God … the ridge is running in me." She gasped as the very real feeling of having someone rub a fingertip along the inside of her bottom struck her for the first time.

"Megan, honey, this is a pretty gentle piece of ginger, but tell me if you get terrible pain or heat from it."

As he passed the ginger root back and forth in her bottom, one hand back playing with her clit now, her spasms began to build, and so did—what? "It's not painful, but … oh … oh it's like, it's like when you have a really bad itch and you need to scratch it or something. It's irritated, I guess." He pulled the root out, but the feeling persisted. "Stephen, please … it still feels … I need something. Is there something you can put in there … something a little larger, I mean like a backscratcher for my ass, I think?"

"I think I can help you, Megan. Easy now." Moving his hands up from her vee to her hips, he held her as his cock pressed hard against her bottom. This time, blessed some by the quick explosion earlier and his constant manipulation of her, she did not panic. There was one moment of pain—she might have screamed some—and then he was in … and my God, he filled her. She thought she was going to explode, but he was just in her, and then he pressed in farther, with a soft moan of his own. "You are so warm and tight, kitten. You are amazing." And then he began to move back and forth in her, as if he were in her pussy, but more slowly.

And my God, she thought, *that is it exactly.* The tightness of her backside, the way he filled her, and the motion back and forth was just the scratch she had needed.

Later, she thought it was just like that moment when you put a Q-tip in your ear and get the exquisite itch, or when you finally raise your top and get at a mosquito bite. At the moment, though, when his hand returned to her engorged clit and he moved in her, she did not think beyond the feeling. She put her head back and screamed a single keening note of enjoyment as her tummy crushed down and her pussy snapped closed on his finger, caught in the grip of a powerful orgasm. As she pressed and relaxed, taken over by the feeling, he began to move faster, and shortly, she felt the brief fire of his explosion in her—a fire that faded, but the delicious pressure in her did not; not until much later, when he pushed himself off of her back and shoulders, which he had collapsed onto, and pulled out of her.

He slid up onto the bed and pulled her around to face him. Before he could speak or move, she looked at him with her green eyes sparkling and said quickly, "Yes, Daddy, under the circumstances, I think I can forgive you." He kissed her and wrestled her around, her laughter ringing to the ceiling.

After getting cleaned in the shower and changing the sheets, she lay nestled against him once again, her bottom tucked against him, his cock a warmth beside her ass, his hand around her, softly cupping one breast. She cast one eye on the clock. "Ten twenty," she mused aloud. "Much better than last night ... I wonder." She began to experimentally wiggle her bottom against him.

His hand reached out and slapped the upper side of her thigh. "Do you really need more punishment, baby doll?"

"Oh please, sir. I know so little, and you know so much." She could not hold back the giggling, but the laughter that followed was all his. As he put her feet on his shoulder and pulled her to him, she glanced at the clock. She was not sure she would see three o'clock again. She was afraid it might kill her—with joy.

34

A Kitten's Valentine's Day

"Daddy." Megan leaned against the door to Stephen's study in a stance that would have drawn him in if he had not known what was really bothering her. She had lifted one foot, placing it against her other shin, raising the hem of the little chemise she had worn to bed the night before high enough to let him know that the panties matched the bright red color of her garment. "Daddy, good morning. Are you going to work today?"

He made a final note on the keyboard, put his hands flat on the desk, and, with neither a smile nor a frown, looked at her and said, "No, kitten. Not today. I thought it was important to spend this entire day with you. I will work from the study a bit. You can come in if you want to, Megan." He knew that was not what she wanted. He heard her mutter "damn" in the hallway as she rattled the doorknob.

She chewed her lip for a minute, and then, in her most careful and charming steps, she floated into his study and lifted the hem of her chemise up to her navel, revealing her panties. "Special for Valentine's Day, Daddy. Do you like the little heart on the front?" she said, pointing to the little lace insert in the very center of the panel "Or the great big heart on the back?" She turned and leaned to touch her ankles, showing a large heart with the word *Daddy* inside it.

He relented enough to let a small smile cross his lips. This was going to be difficult; it always was with her. He wasn't sure if he loved her too much or simply wanted her too much—probably both. "I can't decide such an important question right now, kitten. Why don't you put them on my desk, and I will study the matter." She blanched; clearly she had been hoping to draw him out a little bit. But she did exactly as she was told and slipped the garment down off her ankles and feet and deposited it gently on his desk.

She shifted back and forth for another moment as he pretended to study and then pocket the panties. She then finally whimpered. "Daddy, the bathroom is locked or broken or something. And I really need to go. We had all that soda at the game last night, and … could you please see if you can open it. I went to all the others … they are locked too."

He gave her a hard look and then spoke very quietly. "There are no bathroom privileges for you today, Megan. I think you know why, but we will talk about it when the morning routine is completed. Until then, perhaps you can let me finish this small matter. The sooner I finish, the sooner we can see what we can do to help you. Oh, and kitten, put these on, please." He pulled out a pair of cotton panties with little scalloped edges, all in white—what Megan would term with disdain "little girl panties"—from a desk drawer and tossed them to her.

Megan had been trying since she had woken up with a full bladder and a locked bathroom door to control herself, to please him, to get past this. The panties pushed her, in her distress, past the edge she knew was before her. Her unsheathed foot came down in a small stamp with an angry, "I don't want some little baby's panties; I want to go to the bathroom. I *need* to go to the bathroom. *Please* unlock the door now, Daddy."

He looked at her without reacting, and then said very slowly. "You know that stamping gets you spanked, young lady, as that last one will. But we have other things to deal with, so you will be spanked later. Right now, you have two options. You can be very bad, Megan Kathleen, and pee where you stand—which will end all your privileges for a very long time—or you can put your punishment panties on, and then I will tell you where you can go to the bathroom."

Megan knew she had crossed the line, but she did not know at that minute what she had done to warrant suspension of her bathroom privileges. She only knew that when Daddy got very quiet and started using her full name and words like *young lady*, there was trouble ahead. She took the hated plain panties and started to sit in the visitor's chair in front of his desk to put them on. "No, Megan." His voice had gotten lower—a sure signal that something was wrong. "Put the panties on like any young lady would who was standing before her Daddy and had to be covered. Put them on standing up, please." She harbored some hope that he really wasn't mad, that he just wanted her to be scared as he watched her, before he took her. As the scenario unreeled in her mind, she found herself wiggling into the white panties, already a little wet. But her hopes crashed at his next words.

"You will find a kitty litter pan in the utility room, Megan, next to the washing machine. Mrs. Charon is off today, so that will be your space. Now listen to me very carefully: You may slide your panties down, young lady, but not off, to use the box. After you have used it, be sure to use the scooper to clean it up, and put fresh litter in. And if you have to, Megan, remember to roll the pieces in the litter to kill the odor. Now run along and take care of yourself. When you are done, wait for me if I am not already there."

"*Daddeeee!*" she shrieked. "I *don't want this.*" She threw herself against his desk, crying. He came around the desk to her and took her shoulders in his hands—not the hug she had been looking for.

"This is not easy for me, either, Megan, but you broke important rules, and you need to learn that breaking the rules gets you punished. Now"—he reached down and pulled her chemise up and off of her, her arms coming up as he tugged on the lightweight fabric—"that is how I want you for the rest of the day, young lady. If you don't leave for the litter right now, I will conclude you don't want it, and put it away. And then you will spend the rest of the day cleaning up your messes."

Determined now not to give him the satisfaction of any more tears, she stormed out of the study and made her way to the back of the house, and the utility room.

As her angry steps faded away, he sighed, put down the papers he had been staring at in an unsuccessful attempt to read, and got up to follow her. He stopped in the den, making sure that all the preparations were in order, but all was as it should be. She hadn't made it that far this morning. He found her in the utility room, crying and frustrated. Her panties were halfway down her legs, there was kitty litter everywhere, and urine had run down the inside of her leg. He looked at her and said, "Megan, princess, you are much larger than a feline kitten is. Slide your panties down below your knees, and kneel on either side of the pan, dear."

She wouldn't dignify his words with any comment, although her heart had thumped a little at the word *princess*. He had *never* treated her this way before in the two years she had been his since the all-day-long meeting at the accounting office she had worked in on his accounts, or those of Jackson and Partners—the meeting that had ended in her lying over his knee and getting the first spanking of her adult life, then going home with him, never to go back to the office. So the word *princess* was one thing she seized on in her misery. "Daddy, I can't do this. I just want to go to the bathroom." She nonetheless followed his instructions, and knelt with her knees on either side of the kitty litter. Realizing how she could now pee, she finally yielded to the overwhelming urge, and the stream flowed into the pan. Knowing that he was watching every action just made her blush all the more. But the relief was incredible. As she picked her head up, she spied a roll of toilet paper by the side of the pan. "Daddy, please don't watch."

"I had thought I could trust you, Megan, my love, as an adult. I learned this week that you had not only not earned that trust, but broken it. So I need to take you back to school and teach you a couple lessons. After that, well, we'll see; perhaps there will be some Valentine's Day left. But lessons come first. Wipe yourself, please; we have a lot to address this morning."

Grimacing after policing the area around the pan, the brunette flashed her green eyes once more at him, determined to be as grim and prim as he wanted her. "Where may I dispose of my trash, sir?" she said with enough heat to scorch his clothes.

He pointed across to the wall. "The trash can is where it always is, Megan Kathleen. Use it, please."

As the adorable girl, the very center of his life, got up, she kicked off the hated panties and stepped away. *Megan, stop.* He picked up the soggy garment from the floor and held it out to her. "I did not give you permission to take these off. If I tell you to wear them, you wear them until I tell you otherwise. Is that clear?"

"But Daddy, Stephen, they are *wet.*" The look of distaste on Megan's face would have been comical in other circumstances, set off by her nudity. Now he could only look at her, holding her chin in one hand to speak directly to her. "Then perhaps, Megan, you will recall how important the truth is and learn not to hide things from me again. Now get dressed, clean up here, and meet me in my study."

The study, she thought to herself, *is where punishments get handed out.* "But Daddy, what did I do that has you so mad?"

"Join me in the study, Megan, and we can discuss what you did wrong, and why I am upset. You have several things to answer for, dear. I intend to see that you answer for every one." With that, he turned to go back up the stairs. Megan knew he would check, so she left the room spotless, spat in the kitty litter pan just for good measure, and—with very heavy steps, chafing already at the wet panties as they rubbed against her skin—went upstairs.

Her gaze shifted first to the wall of the study rather than to Stephen, who was standing in the center of the room. And she gave a soft sigh of relief. The crop that he kept there was still in the brackets on the wall. He had bought the crop in the first year after she had moved in, and he had used it on her once, at her request. She had no desire to repeat the experience; it was like having fire poured in a line on her skin. "Daddy?" Megan asked, finally looking at him. "I know you are angry, and I am sorry for what I did, but please, it's Valentine's Day, and I don't want you to be mad at me any longer. Please."

Stephen walked up to her, rested his lips against her forehead, and paused for a minute. Then he led her, gently but firmly, over to the one spot in the room she detested—the blank corner. "Kitten, I am not mad at you, and I love you dearly. But holiday or rainy day, rules are rules. And when you break a big one, kitten, then you get big-time discipline. I am sorry this happened on Valentine's Day, but you should have told me instead of letting me find out on my own. Now, not another word." He placed her head in the undecorated intersection formed by the two walls and then knelt beside his brunette beauty.

"But Daddy, I don't even know wha—"

His finger to her lips cut her off in midsentence. "Either you can learn from your mistakes, miss, or all your work, and mine, has been put to waste. Either you are my kitten, or you are just another pretty accountant. I prefer to think you are my kitten. And in deep need of a lesson." As he talked, he slid the hated, white cotton underpants down to midthigh, leaving her nearly naked facing the wall. The beauty shivered a little bit, knowing she had to hold still for corner time, but not knowing if she could.

She knew when he left her panties right there, sliding them no further, that she was in for real trouble. If he took them off her, she was going over his knee, and that would be that.

But he had a point he wanted to make. He put one hand on her forehead, as if to hold her there. "It's important to me now, Megan, very important, that you say absolutely nothing."

She started as a cold dab of lubricant was placed on her bottom, and then she felt him putting the first bead of a string of large anal beads inside her. She tried to keep it out, then force it out, with her muscles, but he was inexorable, and the lubricant allowed it to slide in. He had warned her about this. Tears started to slide down her cheeks as she stood with her wet panties down on her legs, the awful thing in her butt, and the rest of the beads tapping on her thigh. Life could not get worse. And then he whispered in her ear.

"How did you break the window, Megan?"

Oh my God! The window! It had been two weeks. She had completely forgotten the window, and he had never noticed. She had paid for the repair with cash, so she had just put it out of her mind. How did he know?! When had he found out? "Oh, Daddy—"

As she tried to find a way to tell him, the second bead slid in, and then the third. The fullness was all she could focus on, her entire being centered on the string of plastic beads in her butt. "Daddy, Stephen, please, please, please pull it out … it, it makes me feel so full and ashamed." And that is when the fourth bead slid in, and she dimly felt her muscles begin to cramp down on the pressure—a discomfort she could not deal with.

"Megan, dear, I don't want you to have an accident right here in the corner, but if you don't tell me, right now, exactly how the window was broken, you are going to get this entire string in you. The last time I administered these, you got only three beads." He paused a moment.

"Now, I don't know how much you can take, but I don't want to find out, young lady. So talk." He gave the string a little sideways tug, as if preparing to find out if the next one would fit.

"Oh, Daddy … I broke it playing with Chrissy. She was over and just twirling and twirling—you know how she does—and I picked up your baseball that sits on your desk and threw it at her to get her to stop, but it missed and went right through the window. Oh, Daddy, I am so sorry … please, please, please—" Her voice was cut off completely as the fifth bead went into her. It was big enough on its own to bother her; with the other four, her tummy truly began to cramp. "Daddy, please, I will tell you everything. May I kneel down? My tummy is starting to hurt … I feel so full … I want … I don't know … but please?"

With his kitten pleading and tears coming down her cheeks—rolling down them, in fact, he relented. The largest bead came out with a pop so loud that Megan blushed and squeezed her thighs together … it was like she had farted during an exam. "And how did you get the window replaced so fast, kitten? I was only gone for two days."

"Um … Chrissy called Mike and asked him what a friend should do, and he knew this guy who would come over that day and replace it for two hundred dollars. And it was the start of my allowance, so I had two hundred dollars … and Chrissy promised she would pay for our fun for the rest of the two weeks … so … I said okay. I didn't mean to deceive you, Daddy … I just wanted things to be okay and easy."

"Do you know what would have happened, Megan, if you had called me and told me what had happened?" He was now pulling the sodden tresses of hair away from her face. If he could, he would have taken her in his arms and held her tight, but that would never do; there was a lesson to learn. "Or you could have told Randy, kitten. He was out, but in town."

"If I called you, Daddy, or if I called Randy and then he called you, I would have gotten sent to the bedroom until you got home, and then spanked!" Her upturned, tear-streaked face was twisted in anguish. There was a lot of discipline to go, but he knew she was at the edge right now.

"Probably, kitten. But there would have been just a spanking, and then you would have been back in my arms. As it is—kitten, did you know all our windows are electrified? That there is special glass that carries a current? It's part of our alarm system."

Megan's head swiveled faster than he would have thought possible. "They are, Daddy? I mean, I know there is an alarm system, and you showed me how to activate and deactivate it, and it goes on at night all by itself, but no—I didn't know the windows are electric. How come?"

He knew she was stalling, but he had never been able to resist her wide-open green eyes. "Because, kitten, this is an obvious target for burglars, this house. And while I would not weep for the things inside it, I would never forgive myself if anything happened to you—or to Randy or Mrs. Charon, for that matter. So we have a very advanced alarm system that will bring private security quickly and the police as well. When the cheap glass was put in, kitten, it not only deactivated the alarm; it fried the circuits in the alarm upstairs. Randy actually noticed it when he went upstairs to find some luggage; if he hadn't, there could have been a fire. We were very lucky, Megan. And we would not have had to rely on luck if you had simply told me what had happened. Understand now why I am upset with you?" The last bead slid out of her bottom without a noise, but with a little liquid trail. She was clearly mortified, but she kept her hands at her sides.

"Daddy, I am *so* sorry. I didn't know we had such a snazzy alarm system. You should have told me!"

"Megan Kathleen, don't even start. I cannot imagine every detail ahead of time. When a kitten has a problem, even an accident, it is not a good solution to try to cover it up, even if her friends will help her.

What is the right solution, young lady?" When he tilted her head up to look at him by holding her chin, she knew that things were not at an end.

"I should tell Daddy when that happens, sir."

"Exactly. Now come along, young lady." He took her by the hand and walked her over to the straight chair that had been placed all alone in the middle of the study. She hated that chair. She wanted to be spanked, when she had to be spanked, on the sofa in the den, where she could brace herself. And then she saw what was on the table next to the chair. And suddenly he was dragging her, not walking her along.

"Daddy," she said in little more than a hoarse whisper. "Please no. Don't use the hairbrush. I have learned my lesson … I really have. And I feel miserable; I can still feel those awful beads inside me. I will all day, won't I?"

"You will, kitten. And perhaps you will remember the lesson that you already know. But it's an important lesson, Megan—one you must never forget again. So"—he sat down on the chair and pulled her by the wrist to him—"let's not put it off any longer, shall we?"

"Daddy." She knew what was coming, but she had to try anyway. It could hurt so badly. "Please, not my thighs, not with the hairbrush, please?"

He did not bother to answer her immediately; he merely set himself and pulled her across his lap, centering her, as he always tried to, on his knee, the hard surface forcing her trimmed slit up and out a bit. When she was excited, he liked to tease her in this position. This time, though, he hoped her humiliation might help her to learn this lesson. He set the hairbrush down on the table next to him, quietly, and then, without preliminaries, he connected with a strong open right hand on Megan's bottom. *Crack!*

"*Daddy!*" Megan screamed, because she knew it was expected, but she privately gave a prayer of thanks—it had been only his open hand, and she knew his hand would get tired before too long. As his hand landed again and again on her bottom, she did what she always tried to do—she held onto the chair rung and closed her eyes and dreamed they were somewhere else, someplace on vacation, because she *always* got wet when he spanked her, and it was silly to waste it.

Her dream was shattered when, on the eighth stroke, his hand changed to the hairbrush. *Wham.* She arched her back, her eyes flying wide open and her legs kicking as she tried to squirm away from the direct, unyielding blows of the back of the heavy, dark hairbrush. *"Oowwww, pleeeasee, Daddy …* please …" Screaming and whispering seemed to do no good, but after one last crack on the back of each thigh, the blows she hated worst, he put down the hairbrush and stood Megan back up on her feet. And then tears did start to flow in earnest.

"Daddy … aren't you going to hold me? Daddy, I love you … I am so upset … please?" Each time Megan got spanked, she got a cuddle, her bottom off his lap, his arms around her back. That signaled the end of her punishment and the beginning of their makeup time. This time he just stood and gave her a strong, long embrace.

"Megan, princess, I love you too, dear. But discipline isn't done until the lesson is learned, kitten, and it's not quite learned yet. Now come along; I think that my kitten is a bit soiled and needs a bath. Unless I am much mistaken, your bath is hot and ready so that you can step right in. So come along, young lady." He slid her panties down and off, leaving her totally naked, and led her by the hand down the hallway. He walked past their big bath, with the giant tub where he bathed her when she was playing, and on down to the guest bathroom. This is where Megan usually had to go for a rectal thermometer, if that was her punishment. He ushered the still crying brunette through the door. "Yes, I think this is just right, young lady. We need to get you clean. There is still pee on your leg, and I want you spic and span inside and out; you are going to get a visitor soon."

45

"Stephen, Daddy, you have never, ever punished me this hard before. I don't want to see anybody. Can you please just finish my discipline, and I promise I will just go to bed?"

"I can't do that, punkin, but I promise you, this is someone you want to see. But you want to be clean before the visitor gets here, so into the tub. *Now!*" He gave her a little tap on the butt that she shrank from, but she nevertheless dipped her toe in the water, only to pull it back with a gasp.

"Daddy ... It's hot! Too hot."

"Young lady, this is not a play bath. Now, you can either get in this tub now, or you can sit by the tub while I cut you the three pieces of soap you will need."

"Oh, Daddy, you are *so* mean." Without another squawk, the pretty girl slid into the too-hot water, gasping and shrinking but nonetheless sitting in the tub, her feet drawn up to her bottom, her hands around her knees.

She had tested him on the soap before, when she had, in a kind of blind moment, yelled "Fuck you!" when he gave her an order she found unpleasant. He told her she was long overdue for soap treatment. She had assumed he meant to put a bar of soap in her mouth, as had been done when she was a child. He had warned her differently, but she really hadn't paid attention. While she was in the tub, he cut three pieces off a big bar of soap. Then he told her to get on her hands and knees in the tub, with her back arched and her head up. He popped one piece in her mouth and told her to chew but not swallow. "Chew very slowly," he had said to her. He slid another piece into her bottom, and the third piece he slid into her pussy. He then told her she could not spit and could not swallow until the other two pieces had dissolved. He had made her dip her ass in the hot water of the tub, and he then put his finger in her bottom awhile, pushing the soap around to dissolve it, and he then had done the same in her slit.

She finished a very unhappy kitten and had never crossed that line again. She was not about to now. But this bath was not much better. He thoroughly soaped a fingernail brush and then used it on the inside of her already tender thighs, smiling to her and saying, "We don't want you with pee on your legs when company comes, little one."

It was almost one by the time her bath was winding down. She had had her legs scrubbed, a washcloth on his fingers pushed into her pussy, another washcloth pushed into her bottom, her body scrubbed repeatedly, and her hair washed twice. Although she was exhausted, she fairly glowed from every corner. She had decided the "company" was a story he had made up to embarrass her; he did that sometimes. But then there was a knock at the bathroom door, and without a second thought, he simply said, "Come in, dear."

Megan scrambled to cover herself—her legs had been splayed open after his latest scrubbing—when she saw that it was a sobbing Chrissy that had come in the door. "Chrissy!" Megan shouted, but Stephen gestured to her to be silent, which caught her by surprise.

"Chrissy, dear," Stephen said, "I told Mike to make sure you were embarrassed on the ride over, but I never dreamed he would put you in that silly water-bra outfit. Get that little T-shirt and bra off now, darling; your tits are fine the way they are." And truly, Chrissy was a golden-haired beauty. She had a lithe dancer's body, flawed only by her 36C bust; full lips, and a sweet disposition. She and Megan had been friends since shortly before Stephen and Megan met; they both belonged to the same ski club. Megan had feared that living with Stephen would put an end to their friendship, but it seemed just the opposite.

Chrissy always wanted to be with the two of them, and though she truly cared for her dominant, Mike—coincidentally a friend of Stephen's for years—she really was more comfortable with Stephen. She and Megan had celebrated a little hard one night and started kissing each other in a restaurant. Stephen had simply moved to them, put his arms around them, and said "C'mon, kittens, let's get you some privacy for loving," and he had the bill paid and the limo out front before either one of them could cool off. When he finally convinced them he wanted them to enjoy each other in the car, they had a fabulous night, finally inviting him into bed with them. Since that time, they had shared many more intimate moments together.

Now Chrissy just stood there in the little bathroom, dressed only in a silly little schoolgirl skirt that provoked more than covered. She had moved from tears to sobs, leaving no doubt that Mike had told her why she was being punished. "Oh, Megan," Chrissy managed to sob, "I am so sorry. Mike told me that Stephen had called him and told him not to say anything, to wait and see if either one of us said anything. Honey, I never meant to get you in trouble."

Stephen stood up and lifted Chrissy's chin in a gesture Megan recognized; they were not done yet, and the lead in the pit of her stomach grew. "Chrissy, dear," he said, "do you need a bath?" The blonde's eyes grew wide, and she shook her head in negation. "Then get out of that skirt, dear, so that you are naked like Megan, and dry her off. You ladies have an appointment in the den with me in ten minutes, so be prompt. And come as you are; Randy and Mrs. Charon are gone—it's just the three of us."

"Yes, sir … I will," Chrissy said. "It's just that … that I am supposed to tell you that Mike decided to let you punish me … that I need some kind of punishment. He said you would know." The gorgeous girl dropped her skirt to the ground, leaving her truly naked and beautiful.

"That's fine, Chrissy; it won't change our plans at all. Both of you hurry along now. Nine minutes and counting."

Stephen wasn't all that surprised when the sound of two sets of footsteps stopped just outside the den eight minutes later. "Come in, ladies. Let's get this over with." The door was open, but the women did not enter. Stephen said, "As Megan has pointed out to me, Chrissy, it's Valentine's Day. I have spoken with Mike already, and you will be spending the night with us. So let's see if we can finish discipline before dinner; I have a special Valentine's dinner surprise for the two of you. It would be a shame to waste it on sniffles and sobs."

Megan came around the arched doorway leading into the den, tugging, almost pulling, Chrissy by hand. The pretty blonde turned shy, coyly covering herself and averting her head. "Chrissy, dear ... whatever is the matter?" Stephen asked. "I have held your naked body in my arms before and enjoyed your pleasure, dear one. Is there something wrong?"

Between sobs, Chrissy managed to offer that before, it had been for fun and love and special, but that she had never been punished by him before and was, quite simply, afraid. Punishment was never good with Mike.

"There is nothing to be afraid of, young lady," Stephen said when she had finished. "Come along; let me show you something." He took Chrissy's free hand, and together, Megan and Stephen brought her into the den. It was only when they were in the den that Megan caught her breath in a gasp. Stephen followed her gaze to the crop on the table and smiled. "Chrissy, I want you to hold Megan's hand. Megan, dear, I am going to put the crop back up on the wall in my study. Since this is Chrissy's first time with us, I think the crop would be a little severe. So we will go with something simpler." As he put the crop aside and opened a drawer in the corner table to get a hand paddle, he heard Megan breathe a sigh of relief.

He seated himself on the sofa and then patted his lap. "Chrissy, dear—right over my lap now; let's not fuss about it." Chrissy dropped Megan's hand and made as if to lie over his lap, but she lifted herself with one hand on the couch and said, "You aren't sitting quite right—"

Wham. The paddle cracked down on the very center of her bottom, cutting her off in midsentence with a kind of squeak. "When you are punished in my house, young lady, by my hand, you will be punished the way I say. Now not another word."

With Megan looking on, Chrissy got four more severe strokes with the paddle, and then another five strokes on the curve of her bottom and her thighs, from his hand. As Megan watched her close friend, she watched Chrissy's expression change from one of fear and embarrassment to one of something very different. Stephen continued as if he had not noticed. He stood the pretty blonde up, not paying attention to the way she clenched her thighs together, and pulled Megan to him. "You were here not too long ago, kitten. But fair is fair. Chrissy was spanked in front of you, so …"

Megan, tears streaming, lay over his lap without protest, but she did quietly say, "Please, Daddy, I will never hide anything from you again, I promise."

"I believe that your promise might be worth something after all this time, Megan. But we need to seal the deal." He pulled Megan tight into his lap after the ten-stroke spanking—five with the paddle and five without—and then patted the outside of his lap. Chrissy, dear," he said, "there is plenty of room for you to lie here. I want your head near Megan's feet, Chrissy, and vice versa." It took him a minute to get the girls settled firmly on his lap, with their ends opposed, but finally things were set, and his hand rose and fell again. He stopped counting—the slaps were not hard. And as the girls moved, he suspected that they had moved past discipline.

As he gave each girl a pinch at the center of lovely bottoms that had moved from bright red to dark crimson, he reflected on how fortunate he truly was, and then he said, "All right ladies, I think there has been enough punishment for today." He doubted there was enough room on his lap to hold them both without some small pain to their bottoms, so he led them over to the low bench and had them kneel next to each other. He kissed them both gently, and then harder. "Chrissy, dear, Megan knows how much I love her, and that at the end of discipline comes love and forgiveness—and maybe more. I want you to know that same thing." Kneeling in front of her, he pulled her up onto her knees in a deep hug and gave her a passionate, deep kiss. But he suspected the blonde dancer was ready for more.

After breaking the kiss, she whispered to Megan, "Is it always like this?" At her nod, Chrissy's eyes went wider.

Then Megan said, "Tell him."

"Sir ... um ..." Chrissy bit her lip. "Mr. Ja- ... Daddy? I am *so* wet ... it's never like that with Mike ... he doesn't spank very well, and I have to show him ... and I am never ... oh." She ground her body softly against his in longing.

He simply smiled and took her hand and pulled it to Megan's pussy—and left it there. He knew his kitten. "Are you as wet as Megan is, Chrissy?"

As she gently explored her friend, Chrissy's eyes got bigger. Then she managed to say, blushing deeply, "I know ... I know I am here to be punished ... but could we ... we just ..." Chrissy could go no further, one hand over her own slit now and one hand on Megan's—not in shyness, but in wanting. He laughed, put one girl over each shoulder so they were both hanging down his back, and, after taking a moment to steady himself, walked down the hallway to the bedroom, where he laid the girls gently down on the fresh cotton linens. He started to make a shot at a speech, but the girls were already entwined in each other. Megan lifted her head to say "Daddy, we promise we will never, ever do anything stupid like that and keep it from you again. Now *please* take off your clothes and get down here with us."

"Daddy!" Megan shrieked a few hours later. "They were *so* cold, and you are such an evil man. I thought you meant *chocolate*-coated strawberries!"

He smiled, wiping some juice up from Chrissy's spread legs and pulling the last plump berry out of Megan's spread pussy, having gently inserted it just about five minutes earlier.

"Who wants chocolate-covered berries, Megan, when I can have kitten-coated berries?"

Megan groaned and surrendered her lips to Chrissy, who seemed to have other fruit in mind.

Megan Kathleen Murphy is a successful young accountant at one of the most prestigious firms in the region. She is young, smart, and pretty, with her whole career ahead of her. Professionally, she's satisfied and challenged, but something in her life is ... missing. She yearns for someone to take control, tell her what to do. She longs for Him, the man who will take her hand—and then tell her exactly what she is to do with it. She desires someone who can make her fly.

Stephen Jackson is, by all accounts, a powerful man. He is accustomed to making important decisions quickly, and that confidence serves him well. So when his accountants alert him to a discrepancy involving nearly a million dollars, he demands answers. When he discovers that she is the one who made the million-dollar mistake, he is faced with another of those snap decisions. His decision will alter both their lives irrevocably – in a way she never could have predicted.

Can Megan accept his decision and her discipline?

His business demands are only part of what he requires. Is this strong, desirable man the one who can lead her to her dreams, or will he simply end her career? As is his custom – he gets what he wants but can she be the kitten he desires?

LET THE GAMES BEGIN.

Stephen Jackson earned his JD from George Washington University Law School. He has written for courts and governments, but prefers to write for fun. Stephen lives and writes, and practices law outside of Washington, DC.

PAGETURNER
PRESS AND MEDIA

CPSIA information can be obtained
at www.ICGtesting.com
Printed in the USA
LVHW030610220420
654155LV00002B/496